Selfie

Selfie

Sujatha V

First Edition: December 2019
By ZDP SPECIFICS

ISBN: 978-93-88860-53-6

ZDP Specifics Title : 3

ZDP SPECIFICS
An imprint of Zero Degree Publishing
No.55(7), R Block, 6th Avenue,
Anna Nagar,
Chennai - 600 040

Website: www.zerodegreepublishing.com
E Mail id: zerodegreepublishing@gmail.com
Phone : 98400 65000

Cover Art by B. R. Srinivasan
Typeset by Vidhya Velayudham

Dedication

Dedicated to my father Late M. Velayudham who was always super proud of his daughter in whatever she did.

Acknowledgements

Thank you would be a very small word for these people in my life, but I don't have an option to express my gratitude in any other manner here.

My sincere thanks to my darling son Naveen, who has been my pillar of strength in every endeavor. Whenever he says "Mom I know you can!" I get really charged on seeing his belief in me.

Thanks to my parents Velayudham and Swarnambal, brothers Balaraman and Jaikumar, sisters-in-law Sumathi and Jaya and niece and nephew , all of whom have always given me the best comfort that a family can give. They have always supported me in anything I do, and it is because of them that I am what I am today.

Thanks to my friend Vijai, who has patiently read all my scribbles. With his inputs and feedback, I could develop it into proper content for this book. Getting the comment "good" from him is very difficult.

Thanks to my friend and publisher Ramjee, who believed in my writing and couraged me beyond my beliefs to publish this book. If not for him, this would have been a distant dream.

Introduction

'Awareness is virtue, unawareness is sin and it is applicable to your whole life' - Osho

'True happiness is not derived from wealth or fame but it lies within us' - Zen Buddhist

They all teach us to become more aware of our thoughts to live a peaceful and happy life. Becoming aware of our thoughts is a big goal. Any goal has to have a beginning of implementation if at all you want to achieve.

'A journey of a thousand miles begins with a single step' – Lao Tzu

I started analyzing how my thought pattern works when I come across various situation. This became an interesting hobby, analyzing a situation and deriving a meaning out of it. I started to write down my thought pattern so that I can review whenever I can. This book is a collection of various situation I came across in my day today life, my thought pattern in those situation and what I implemented to make me a better person day by day. I realized it is a very interesting hobby I had picked up.

Once we start analyzing our thoughts there are so many changes that happens within us. We always live with a constant watch now. It definitely slows you down on the thought level. We think before we speak, before we act and hence we start seeing things clearly. Mind is open to suggestion as we understand that we can't be right always. Believe me it definitely makes you a better person.

This books has my thought pattern and my analysis of various things I came across. As mind wanders, the analysis would be very scattered. I would recommend to read one topic at a time analyze if you have come across some similar situation and how you dealt with it.

Hope this would help in some way towards "**Self Analysis**"

1

Life in Entirety

A few years ago, I was promoting my interior designing project to a potential customer. For some reason, I did not get the project, and we parted cordially. Subsequently, I learnt a lot, developed my career, achieved some milestones, bettered some personal records, and have become a director of a private limited company.

Three years later, I happened to meet this lady again. She recognized me and smilingly asked, "How many customers you are working with right now?" The question was very genuine. But I could not give a simple answer in numbers, simply because my profile had changed. By then, my work was measured in terms of the size of our projects, projects pertaining to the company in which I was (and am) a director.

I tried telling this to her, but possibly she could not grasp it. She gave a sorry smile and from what I read from her face – "So you are still struggling to take projects!" Without further explanation, I left with a brave face.

On my way back home, unable to take that sorry smile, I felt a little restless. I reached home and my helper opened the door. I sat on the sofa, still feeling a little uncomfortable about this unexpected interaction. I wondered if I could even explain my personal growth and achievements to my helper in a manner that she could understand and appreciate. Even if Sachin Tendulkar met my helper and said that he played cricket, she would be likely to think, "Still playing cricket, not doing anything worthwhile." This idea dissipated my cloudy thoughts and calmed my mind.

With a becalmed mind, I realized that each of us views, understands and deciphers words, instances and persons to the extent of our personal maturity, experiences, exposure and biases, never in entirety. The story of six blind men asked to describe an elephant after they have touched different parts of its body is a simple example.

Often, when I hear or read something which I have already heard, I get a deeper insight and process it differently because my exposure and maturity have changed. When my mother said, "Hard work is the key to success, "I treated it as a familiar preaching. But today, when I hear the same words, I appreciate it better and realize its significance, not because the phrase has changed but my maturity with which I listen has changed As I write this, I understand that knowledge is a bottomless pit.

This insight brings the realization that I perceive life only to the extent of my understanding and my maturity, never in entirety - The extent to which I love somebody, to that extent, I understand love. The extent to which I relate with people, I understand relationship. To the extent I parent my son, to that extent I understand parenting. To the extent I manage our organization, I understand management. To the extent I surrender, I understand GOD.

This brings another insight: There are still many things I am yet to try, and I will never understand those things till I get a chance to experience them.

Any game becomes more interesting only when you play more. The more you understand the rules, the more you implement them, the longer you play, you reach a state where anything about the game excites you. Similarly, to play the game of life with ease, peace and happiness, we need to master the rules of the game.

Now it is totally clear that our life is in our hands. All we need to do with every passing day, with every passing experience, is to grow in maturity and imbibe life's lessons. We should strive to learn as much as we can every minute, strive to implement as much as we can and strive to grab more each passing day as every day we live has a purpose and we are not aware of the purpose.

2

Expression

Why do most people eagerly anticipate their birthdays? I can understand children getting excited about their birthdays eager to grow up, looking forward to gifts, but I also saw my father's joy when we celebrated his sixty fifth birthday. This demonstrates that age doesn't matter. Whether their age is seven or seventy, people love to be the centre of attraction. When your loved ones come to meet and greet you on your birthday, hug you tight, pat your back, bring you gifts, they bring you joy that makes your day. What makes a person feel emotional and very happy is these genuine feelings which are demonstrated. If it is so easy to spread joy, the big question is: Why is every day not a birthday?

My niece, just five years old, is a nightmare to my parents. Their regular complaint is "She never listens to anything we say." But whenever I meet her, she becomes a very sweet and obedient girl, happy to prove that she is an angel (which she actually is). My mother usually comments "Ha! She is auntie's girl." I just smile, knowing very well why she behaves like an angel for me while displaying another angle to others. Right through my communication with her, I use words like "My Cinderella is a good girl." I would appreciate her paintings with wide eyes, ask if she really did it and tell her they are just wo..oonderful. She appreciates the attention and gets excited. If it so easy, the big question is: Why is she not excited all the time?

When my staff member's daughter had a health issue, I called her and said, "Don't worry. Your daughter will be fine. If you need any help any time give me a call and I'll be there." When she rejoined office, the first thing she said with tears in her eyes was, "Thanks for your phone call Ma'am. It gave me a lot of confidence that I have a support to fall back on." I could understand what she had gone through. If such reassurance is adequate for a person to feel confident, the big question is: Why are people not feeling secure all the time?

Wherever I go shopping or travelling with my mother, I see her talking so comfortably with people around. By the end of a train journey, she will surely have a couple of co-passengers saying bye, giving their mobile numbers, inviting her home. In my opinion, this is a precious trait we lost as we grew in education, sophistication, white-collar behaviour, and fear of getting cheated. We think twice even to smile at a stranger.

People are waiting for words. Right words at the right time, with the right emotion is the key to success in all the roles we play in life. We are surrounded by people all the time, but very rarely do we get to hear genuine words of appreciation which express love, which say, "I understand," "I care." Most of the time it's taken for granted, and adult behaviour and maturity are expected from us.

If we want to keep our loved ones happy, we need to first ask ourselves: Am I talking from my heart adequately? Am I expressing my love repeatedly? Am I listening to them? Am I communicating "I care," "I understand" language in my gestures, in a way they understand? Of course we have immense love for those who are close to us. But are we demonstrating it with shared joyful time, undivided attention, positive feedback, gentle reproach, pats, hugs, genuine compliments, body language…? A little change in our expressions can make the world for those we love. Let's learn the art of expressing our feelings and create heaven around us.

3

The Hidden Force

Anita, born and brought up in a village, studied in the only elementary school in her village, a school which ended at 8th standard. Her parents, determined to educate her further, took a house on rent in a nearby town, where she completed 12th standard in a government school. Then her parents got her admitted in a college in the same town, where she graduated. Very typical of a village scenario, her parents now wanted her to get some job, get married and settle down.

After a friend guided Anita that one could earn a huge amount in a multinational company on completing MCA, Anita started thinking about her life. When she sought her parents' permission to join the MCA course, they refused. She persevered, somehow got a seat in MCA in a nearby city and informed her parents. With no choice, her parents reluctantly said "Do whatever you want." In the city, it was a struggle to live all alone, especially without her family and with her village background. But she realized, her life would be no different from that of her parents unless she persevered. Even with her MCA qualification, she struggled for a suitable job for two years; her parents' negative comments led her to believe that she had made a wrong decision.

Finally, the breakthrough happened. She got her dream job in an MNC, a huge salary, plus opportunities to travel abroad. Now she became the decision maker. She decides where she wants to live, what she wants to wear, the type of bridegroom she will accept, what she needs for her wedding. Even in the so-called orthodox village culture, her family and everybody else looks up to her and accepts her the way she is.

What I don't understand is the term 'Women's Liberation'. Who has to liberate women and from what? What stops a woman from doing what she wants to do? Who needs to give permission? When a woman decides to do something useful in life, I don't think any power can stop her.

Just imagine, if God tells a man I'll give you enough wealth and take care of your needs, no man would be interested to work. He'll be happy to sit at home, have four servants to do some chores and perform mundane activities to spend his time, sleep in the afternoon, enjoy raising kids, watching TV. Who would decline this kind of lifestyle? Similarly, maybe women just accept their traditional default role of caregivers and never decide what they can do or want to do. Man doesn't give himself an alternative choice but to be an earning member and moreover God is keeping his mouth shut.

While reading Civics with my son, we were trying to decipher the population chart. It stated that people in the age bracket of 20 to 60 years are active members and the rest have to be taken care of by these active members. The age bracket of 20 to 60 was segregated into female and male. This information gave me a sense of uneasiness as I'm sure that a large percentage of the female population is not actually active. I have not considered the major contribution and value of ladies, including those who are employed, to running households, teaching children, etc. Our country can grow at double the present pace if we can convert the inactive (female) group and make it active. I also hope that the home responsibilities will be shared by the husbands of working women.

People in the age bracket of 20 to 60 should first become financially independent. Innumerable women in India have made it to the top. Right from Sheila Dixit to Saina Nehwal, the list is endless and they have succeeded in varied fields. As my teacher often said, "What is possible for one human being is possible for everyone." Every woman should stop depending on male, be it father, brother, husband or son for her basic needs. One has to struggle to earn in crores. But to earn for your basic needs, just a will to begin is needed. Start from where you can start and the path will definitely unfold. I understand that a woman has innumerable responsibilities at home. But never forget your responsibility towards your country. Social service does not necessarily mean that we donate something. When we fulfill our responsibility with maximum effort and strive to improve in every way, that is a bigger service to the nation.

"Give a man a fish and you have fed him for today. Teach a man to fish and you have fed him for a lifetime"—Author unknown. Let us target the dormant segment and teach them to fish. That will be our contribution to our nation.

4

MY FEELING

Summers are always welcome for students as they are guaranteed holidays, and for their parents, who can now spend more time with the children. During the year, at any given time I'll want my son to do something useful, while he'll want to enjoy and chill. Hence I decided that I will accept whatever my son plans during his summer holidays. When he wanted to go abroad, I accepted. After much discussion, we decided to visit Singapore and Malaysia. Planning, packing, organizing was so much fun and he was so excited on the day we started.

The holiday was so thoroughly exciting and enjoyable. My brother suggested that we also visit Langkawi. I vaguely knew it to be a bunch of islands near Malaysia. When we started early in the morning, it was drizzling and the entire route to the ferry station was so beautiful with abundant trees and greenery. 90 minutes after the ferry started, we had reached Langkawi. The ferry was completely air-conditioned and I chose not to look out during the journey. Coming out of the ferry, I was wowed by the beautiful scene I saw. The place was so beautiful with hills, islands, streams surrounded by the sea.

Moving around Langkawi, I thought God has been very partial here, creating a heaven on Earth. I understood the word "breathtaking" as we went up by cable car. Standing there 700 metres above sea level, we were standing in the clouds and this was truly a WOW moment for all of us. The green thick forest below, the vast expanse of the sea, the small islands, the waterfall far far below… Standing there, I realized that any number of words could never explain how peaceful and excited I felt about Langkawi. How I felt is very personal to me and I can never explain completely the way I felt. People can understand that it is a beautiful place worth seeing, nothing more.

When I can't even explain my feelings about a place that exists, can be seen and that I have visited, how can I fully explain my feelings for anybody? I could say, "I love you so much," but can that explain the depth of my feelings? I can talk so much about my feelings but words are insufficient. No matter how much I tell my parents they mean so much to me, mere words can never fully express the overwhelming gratitude which flows inside. Feelings are very personal and can never be expressed by mere words.

Even while studying, my son will suddenly ask, "Hey, do you love me?" I used to ask him why he asked this suddenly and repeatedly, but he would insist on a reply. But after realizing that I won't be able to explain my exact feeling in words, I understood that he is trying to understand my feelings. My feelings are mine alone, very personal and internal, and can't be explained. So I just smile, give him a hug and repeat that he means the world to me. So is the case with one's feeling towards God. You can visit places of worship, sing hymns, prayers, do rituals and wear amulets, but can anything explain what you feel for your God.

Just when we think we have understood everything, we suddenly realize we don't even understand the feelings of others. This is what makes life so beautiful. A feeling is something which you hold inside. It is born inside you, cherished by you alone and perishes with you. That is why, when words are not enough to explain yourself, tears emerge. Tears of joy, tears of gratitude, tears of sadness bring out the expression of feelings deep inside. Don't be upset when people don't understand your feelings. They are yours and yours only.

5

Dreams – Beware

An incorrigible dreamer, I have a habit of living in a fairyland where everything appears perfect. In flashback mode, I could draw a lot of parallels between my dream world (DW) and the real world (RW).

DW: As a youngster, I used admire movie heroines. Their walk, talk, dress and confidence inspired me and I always wanted be like them. I wanted to wear pants, be fluent in English, be very courageous (which I was not) and it remained part of my DW.

RW: I had to join a hostel for my engineering degree. The friends' circle I got associated with had a lot of influence in my growing years. I picked up their language, their lingo and dress style. I had to be confident to survive in the group without the support of parents, which built my personality and greatly contributed to my current avatar.

Merger: Somewhere the dream world and real world merged and I became the person I saw in the dream world.

DW: As a little girl, I had much interest in Art and loved dancing, painting, art work. I used to imagine myself performing or creating something all the time.

RW: After becoming an Engineer I first worked in the software industry, where I always aspired to improve my software proficiency. By chance I got into the designing field and today I am an established designer, which gives me a platform to be creative.

Merger: Somewhere the dream world and the real world merged and I became the person I saw in the dream world

DW: Shortly after joining the software industry, I bumped into a group of classmates. During my casual discussion, I said after 10 years I want to be on my own and do some business. I used to imagine myself in a big office, highly qualified to give solutions to any office problems and live in style.

RW: Exactly after 10 years I started my own organization with a lot of trepidation. Today I am a happy business owner.

Merger: Somewhere the dream world and the real world merged and I became the person I saw in the dream world.

DW: I imagined myself as a darling mother who epitomizes love.

RW: Exams, keyboard, tennis class, behaviour, attitude, cleanliness, eating habits …sometimes I thought I'll be only a terror to my son, always with an instruction.

Merger: During one of our intimate conversations, my son said, "I need only you and I'll earn everything else in my life" very casually. I realized beyond the do's and don'ts the dream world mother and the real world mother had merged and I had became the mother I saw in the dream world.

The list goes on and on. This brings the realization that I have a responsibility even towards my dreams because I'm convinced that one day they will come true. The life which I see in my dreams today is the guiding path to my future. God sees my dreams and plans my life accordingly. I better become aware of my dreams.

6

DIVINE LOVE

I phoned my uncle to wish him on his birthday.

Me: Love you Uncle

Uncle: I love you Suja

Me: Happy Birthday, Uncle

Uncle: Thank you ma. Love you so much. Thanks for remembering.

After disconnecting the call, I pondered how comfortably I use the magic words "I love you" and it has become an integral part of my communication:

I still remember that during my childhood, the word LOVE was a banned word at home. In our home, LOVE was understood in a very wrong sense, since it was usually heard in the context of love letter, love marriage and (blush blush) lover. In fact I used to blush when I heard anybody use this word. Love was defined as a feeling between two adolescent people and it was portrayed as a crime.

It is hence natural that in the environment I grew in, one could never boldly say "I love …", and I followed this rule until I met my teacher. He gave a new dimension to the word LOVE. Anybody who meets him would get a hug & a whisper "love you so much" and I saw the impact it created on me as well as others. As my maturity developed, I understood that love can melt anybody's heart. It is associated with divinity. It is love that makes this world a sensible place to live in. It is my love for my parents that urges me to become a good daughter, my love for my son that urges me to become a good mother, my love for my work that makes me a better designer, my love for fellow humans that makes me forgive people who hurt me, my love for my teacher that makes me listen to what he says. It's my love for life that gives me a purpose to live one more day of my life usefully.

Love is eternal. Nehru may have so done much for the country but his love for children is our outstanding memory. Mother Teresa's love for fellow humans is the root of Missionaries of Charity. The unconditional love a mother has for her children is what makes motherhood so special. When you encounter a challenge, it's your love for God which makes you say "He is giving me an experience to grow." Meera's love for Krishna raised her to a saintly position. Jesus preached "Love All", which is the beginning of Christianity.

Once you start expressing your love unconditionally, you begin to experience peace within. I can't change my childhood, but definitely I can influence the next generation and cultivate the feeling that love is divine. Experientially we can make people realize that love is divine, because it is. At times my son and I fight like cat and dog. We stop talking to each other. But before going to bed, we have a habit of saying "Love you so much," which obviously brings smiles and lightens our hearts. Next day heralds a new beginning.

At home I have inculcated a habit; the moment I walk in, the little ones come running with open arms, shouting "huggie". The tight hugs with so much love and the "love you" makes them feel very secure and I see that they feel very comfortable with me. When we approach children with love, they are more likely to heed to our words. Any other approach only creates resistance.

Love is the only means to lead a peaceful and blissful life. Let us not have a wrong perception of love. Let us not hesitate to express our love for people. Let us not blush and miss out on a divine experience. Let us practise unconditional love to every form of life on earth and feel the divinity within.

7

Transcendence

I heard this word for the first time when my teacher used it in class, and was unsure if I had understood its meaning based on context. Next day, it was still harping on my mind and so I checked the Internet to know the meaning. But the Internet definition convinced me that I had not grasped its correct meaning. Yet for 16 years my experience had led me to believe that I understood everything the teacher said, so the description as understood by me was right. This definition of transcendence was: **"Giving up the ones which you like or love, but still managing to live happily and blissfully."**

I grew up as a typical girl where even the words "chocolate" and "ice cream" would make my mouth water. In our joint family, everybody knew these items would bring a smile to my face. I had no shortage of chocolates and ice creams during my growing years. When I started working, I thought that as an adult, I should stop gorging on chocolates. Over a period of time, I was pleasantly surprised to see that for weeks together I could abstain from chocolates that I had loaded in the fridge. It's not that I didn't like chocolates any longer; it's just that I no longer found them enticing. I took my son to an ice-cream parlour, bought him an ice-cream, sat next to him watching him eat and feeling happy. I asked myself, "Why didn't you buy an ice-cream for yourself?" but had no answer. I simply did not crave for it. I now redefined transcendence as **"When you have abundant of something which you like, you no more need it to be happy in life"**

My teacher asked us to play will power improvement games, in which you have to give up something very close to your heart just for a week, which improves your will power. I challenged myself not to eat any cooked food for a week. But karma works only during such times and we had a marriage in the family. Every time I saw food, I told myself, next week I'll eat three times more and make up for all the loss. By sticking to my challenge I was very happy I had improved my will power. But then I realized that the game had improved my will power, but to transcend temptation, I should not feel tempted even at the mind level. Then my definition of transcendence was refined as, **"When giving up something which we like doesn't hurt even at the thought level then it is transcendence"**

When we learn to give up something to rise in life, it shouldn't hurt when you lose your sleep. It shouldn't hurt when you have to say sorry to your loved ones. It shouldn't hurt when your colleague becomes close to your boss and you get sidelined. It shouldn't hurt when the food is not to your liking. A setback in one project shouldn't stop you from doing the next project with the same commitment. Wherever we feel disturbed, we have to analyze the root cause and work towards its transcendence. Then we gradually evolve to a state where nothing can disturb ME, the enlivening force; that's true transcendence. I'm still working on getting still deeper meanings of **TRANSCENDENCE**.

8

Let Go Gracefully

Oh what fun it is to furnish a house for a client. It starts from the functionality of the house - compulsory needs, optional requirements, vaastu requirements, luxuries and add-ons. Get up from here, move around like this, need this here, etc. Once the functionality is in place, we want the house to be unique and with the best ambience. This curtain is perfect, this sofa with those cushions will look neat. Oh that painting in the middle should have this theme… The list is endless. Sweating for months together has made the house that was created in the mind. After so much hard work, finally the house becomes a home exactly as it was visualized or even better and the grahapravesh (housewarming) is fixed.

On the day of grahapravesh, there is no time to even eat, as there are a lot of last minute settings to be done before the guests arrive. At the function, I pick up a bouquet, walk in to the house, hand it to the owner, wish her luck with a smile and walk out gently for I know it's no more "my" house. Next day I feel a part of me is missing, but life moves on and there comes the next project; Get up from here, move around like this, need this here, etc.

In life, anything which starts will end sooner or later. We have this etched in our system when it comes to education and career. We can't keep sitting in 1st standard just because we like it. 1st standard will end one day. We know very clearly it will end even on the day we start. We have prepared our mind to let go that 1st standard when we go the next standard, to let go that class teacher when we meet the next class teacher, to let go that position in the office when we take up higher roles, let go that employee when he decides to leave.

Do we extend this to all facets of life? That is the big question.

Yes you love dancing. Your heart dances when you dance. But are you prepared to stop dancing when it is time to leave? The reasons could be some physical illness or some situation or even because of age. Do you have the maturity to let go gracefully?

Yes, you brought your son up. You shaped his every atom; 25 years of your efforts resulted in the handsome talented young man in front of you. Now he has a mind of his own, plans for his life, for privacy, for a career of his choice. If you still believe that he is yours, will do what you tell him, has no secrets from you, you are wrong and you'll feel the pain when he wants to break free. Are you prepared to let go gracefully?

It's definitely not easy to let go of something or someone we have grown accustomed to. It could be a relationship, a spouse, a skill, a belief, physical faculties, your own small world. It definitely pains, but there may be no choice. We are very clear when it comes to our jobs and careers. Once we extend this understanding to every aspect of life, our lives can be lot more peaceful. There is nothing that is permanently ours. Accept that anything that begins will end one day. The only thing we can do is live every minute enjoying every bit of what we have so that it doesn't hurt much when we have to let it go. Just hold on to the belief that we clear off something so that it can be filled with something else. Learn to let go. Let go gracefully.

9

Blueprint

An old friend phoned and agreed to visit me for dinner with her family. The minute I kept the phone down, my mind was spinning on all that needed to be done: Menu, gifts, how to keep her entertained through the evening, and so on. I mentally finished cooking, planning, shopping... in 30 minutes, then checked if I had planned the entire evening properly. When she arrived with her family, I played a good hostess as I had played it many times in my mind. Everything happened as I had planned and I felt very happy and satisfied about the whole thing.

After she left, I realized that our actions and words begin with thoughts, which are mental pictures. Generated in the mind, rehearsed, planned, lived and only then they become reality. Before I even say anything, I visualize it, only then it is manifested as actions or words. The life we are living today is based on the thoughts which were generated earlier. Things are always created twice; the first time in the workshop of the mind, then in reality. This is what becoming aware of, becoming conscious of, is all about.

An architect releases architectural drawings as blueprints. A blueprint is an ammonia copy of the tracing sheet, which we can call the master copy. If any corrections are necessary, the tracing sheet is corrected and dated, then a fresh blueprint is taken, say Version 2. Directly correcting the blueprint is futile; the correction is visible and mars the neatness, in addition to raising the doubt if the correction is authentic. Most importantly, since the tracing sheet was not corrected, the next blueprint (I cannot even call it "copy") will not have the corrections needed, and there will be 2 or more versions with the same date, creating confusion. We need to correct the tracing sheet to correct the errors permanently. When the tracing is corrected, subsequent blueprints are automatically correct.

I could draw a parallel of the blueprint with our lives. When we see suffering in our life we generally try to work on the situation, the people or our action, not realizing that we are trying to correct the blueprint directly and expect everything to become right. When we see a pattern to our suffering in life, we have to see the pattern of our thinking. If we want permanent solutions to our suffering, we have to correct the tracing – the source – which is our mind. Our mind is our factory which manufactures our destiny. Without correcting the mind, we can't set our life on track.

Understanding this gives us the good news that we are sole owners of our factory and we have complete control over it. Before we even attempt to set life goals, we need to take some mandatory steps. First and foremost is cleaning up. Removal of negative thoughts is the first step before planning big. Becoming aware of our thoughts enables us to distinguish between positive and negative thoughts. With this awareness, we can begin cleaning up, then set mental targets or goals, which should be challengingly high, so that you have to work harder to achieve them and arrive early at your goals. Now the most important thing is to start living your life in the glory of your imagination of the future and not in the memories or suffering of the past. In the process without your knowledge the tracing becomes right and you can be assured that blueprint – your life will automatically become right.

10

Soul mate

Sheela was three years old when she joined school. Asked what she liked about her school, "Friends" was the reply. She loved playing and talking to them all the time. When she was ten years old, she had a large circle of friends. A few close friends, a few best friends. She loved chatting with them and enjoyed every bit of it. When she was fourteen, she had a few friends with whom she shared her secrets. When she completed her schooling, she greatly missed her classmates. On joining college, she made a new circle of friends. Communication with her school friends slowly decreased and she realized her world had changed. While leaving college, again the same promises were made, "We'll be in touch." But as she settled down in a job, got married and life became a little more serious, she found little or no time to miss her friends.

As older friends kept fading away from her life, she still had one relationship which remained evergreen. Whenever she was happy or sad, her first action would be to run to this relationship. She held on to this relationship for it gave her the required comfort in the midst of her busy life. It was not just a rosy relationship, but rather an extension of her own life. She could be just herself without any mask. She could just be happy, emotional, sad or even shout her feelings out. She often feared that this precious relationship was coming to an end, but luckily, it flourished in spite of all their differences. Years rolled by and this relationship remained her pillar of strength and enabled her to prosper. She realized that she has grown to a point where her love for the other is beyond her. The sheer joy of their mutual love nourished their relationship on and she realized she had found her 'Soul mate'.

Each of us seeks at least one such relationship in our lives. The search begins right from birth where in the presence of the other person we feel complete. This relationship could be anybody: mother, father, brother, aunt, uncle, spouse, friend. Often, when you start a sentence, the other will complete it. You think and the other speaks it. It definitely does not come 'Boom' from somewhere. It depends on how much patience both of you have in building this cherished relationship. It necessarily need not be that we speak the other person's language but we learn to understand the other perfectly well. With the frequency that matches and in spite of the differences between the two, you know the other completes you.

Lucky are those who have found and retained such relationships. But it is definitely ok if you are yet to find your soul mate, because you are not alone. Just be true to your own self in any relationship you wish to nourish and cherish. Analyze what you can give in that relationship rather than what you'll get from it. You need this relationship not for any security reasons, but for the joy in loving, in sharing, in giving and most importantly, the joy of being that source of strength to somebody in life with which they live a beautiful life. If we can be that person even to one life then we had lived a very purposeful life.

11

Redefine Happiness

On a fine Saturday evening, a client called to cancel her appointment, which was scheduled in an hour. Realizing that I was free for the evening, I instantly decided to visit the club and give my son a surprise by turning up at his tennis class, which I had been unable to do since quite some time.

I was happily sitting in the shade watching him practice. Next to me were two ladies in their sixties, encouraging their ward with loud cheers and suggestions. I had no choice but to listen to comments like "Super shot," "Kanna well done." One of them said "See how he's sweating. Good for him." The other said, "I knew you'll enjoy this. That's why I wanted you to come." Both were enjoying the class so much that I was curious to see who the child was being cheered. Seeing a small boy just in his beginning stage in the court, I wondered if Rafel Nadal's grandmother would have enjoyed his game so much. I couldn't help but admire these two women.

When my son was sent to another court, I shifted my place. Here an old man was complaining to a nearby parent, "I have become too old. Still I have to take care of these kids. I don't know when their parents will understand that I also need some rest. Blah blah. May be he was too tired to sit through the class. But I still thought 'You are doing it anyway, might as well enjoy it'. I felt like telling him that if you can't be happy in your current situation you can never be happy in any situation.

Once when I saw my son worried. I asked him what the problem was. He replied that for every small disagreement, his friend would threateningly say, "Then you are not my friend." I told him, "This is very simple thing to handle. Next time he tells you that, tell him thank you. Be exaggeratedly happy with your other friends and just ignore him." After a few days, my son happily said, "Oh! Your advice worked! Now he is scared that I'll live happily without him. He wants to be my friend." The world seeks happy people, people with self-confidence.

Happiness is not a destination which you need to reach but a journey. You cannot define happiness. You cannot decide and make a person happy. First one has to learn to be happy in any situation. I have heard people say, "I'll earn lots, buy a house, buy a car and finally settle happily in life." Oh no. It doesn't happen that way. It happens only in fairy tales where they always live happily ever after. The way to the picnic should be as pleasurable as the picnic itself. You can never become happy FINALLY. Happiness is a state of mind to be found and appreciated at all times. It is said that when Birbal was once asked why he was always happy, he replied, "When I wake up, I am happy that God has given me one more day to live, that he has given me health and happiness. When I go out for my morning ablutions, I feel light and refreshed, happy that I am not constipated. And this attitude keeps me happy and contented always."

Decide to be happy in life. You can set any goals in your life – at school, at work, at home. You can achieve your goals only when you work happily towards them. There has to be zest in everything you do. The key to our happiness can never be shared. The world will live its life. If we try to link our happiness with that of others, we can be sure that we will be eternally waiting to be happy. Nobody or nothing deserves your happiness. Redefine your happiness. Make happiness your way of life.

12

Can I Trust You?

Sham, sitting alone, was feeling very lonely. His mind was in flashback mode, remembering his life, his late wife, and regretting their wrong choices. Tears trickled down uncontrollably as he acknowledged that he had spurned a heavenly existence; rather, he had destroyed it with repeated wrong choices and now lived a meaningless life full of regrets.

40 years ago, he and Saradha were married. Their hearts were brimming with joy and they decided to lead the lives of a role model couple. It was great fun living with Saradha. Her every smile filled him with renewed energy. They loved each other totally and would do anything for each other.

When a close friend came from the US and invited Sham to a bar, he accepted, not knowing how to politely refuse. He called Saradha and told her he had some urgent office work and would be late coming home. Three days later, at a get together, Saradha met that friend and learnt of

Sham getting drunk. Unable to bear the thought of Sham lying to her, she cried for three days and told him repeatedly that she could not handle his lying to her. Sham promised never to repeat this act. She trusted Sham and they continued to live in peace.

When her mother called Saradha for shopping at a famous mall, she wanted to inform Sham but absentmindedly forgot. When she spotted Sham in the mall, she happily called him on his mobile. Sham took the call and quickly said, "I'm in a meeting. I'll call you later," and cut the call. But Saradha could see him sitting and chatting with a lady in a coffee shop. When she asked him about this untruth when he returned home, he said, "I thought you would be angry because of your possessiveness and I didn't want to spoil your mood," then continued, "Why did you visit the mall without telling me?" and the argument continued. After fighting on the same topic for about a week, again he promised that he would never ever lie to her. She trusted him once again and life continued.

Sham continued to hide facts, thinking he was protecting Saradha, then his lie would be found and he would promise not to repeat it: this became their way of life. Saradha could no longer trust him, even when he was not lying. If Sham said, "I went to meet a client," she would want to confirm it. She started asking him too many questions which irritated Sham no end. So when Sham said, "You mean a lot to me," she wondered if this so-called affection was to conceal something. The hurt caused by getting cheated repeatedly was too much for her to handle. The more she discussed this with Sham, the more adamantly he defended his truths and untruths, and the less she could believe him. Unable to handle the pressure any longer, she committed suicide and Sham was thrown into darkness. Though he married again and lived his humdrum life, he knew there was a vacuum in his heart that could never be filled.

You have good people around you who live for your sake. Don't ever shake the roots of the trust which they have on you. If you mean everything to a person, you have to think for the other person as well, because they will either live or die holding you. Wake up before it's too late. They might never like certain things about you but when you are honest with them surely they'll accept you with your flaws. When you are honest you help to build a lot of trust in a relationship. With this trust in place you can build anything. If a relationship breaks because of your honesty, it was never a stable relationship. Never ever do anything to shake the trust of the loved ones who live for you and matter to you. Never lose a relationship because it's very difficult to build or repair one.

13

Behind the Scenes

On a fine Sunday morning, I attended the inauguration of a friend's showroom. At the venue, I saw the visibly happy host couple. The guests were awed by the showroom. I could overhear comments like, "He is been lucky all through."

My mind went back. 30 days ago, he had called me and said, "I have to set up a new showroom. What time can we meet today?" He was very clear that he wanted to meet me immediately and I didn't have a choice. When we met, I realized he had exactly 30 days to set up his showroom in a new location. I cautioned him to have a backup plan. We planned for 30 days, but I was also continuously planning the backup. As D-day was nearing, I could see his increasing tension. I had never before seen him lose his cool or raise his voice in anger, but I could see both in those last few days. He was literally eating, sleeping, breathing the project.

Finally the showroom was perfect and inaugurated on schedule. I knew and applauded his efforts and success which made him stand there with pride and joy. He was willing to challenge himself, to go through those sleepless nights, carry the butterflies in his stomach all the time, and all his efforts had paid off. I was also very sure that at the end of the function, he would sit with his team to plan for the showroom's regular operation and continue to set even more challenging targets.

It needs a tremendous mindset to push oneself. Setting and chasing your own goals, leaving your comfort zone and operating in the transition phase is not easy. We all see the final outcome, the limelight and wish we were there. But what we don't see is the enormous effort spent to be in the limelight. Everything has its own challenges. You need to be in Ratan Tata's shoes to understand what it means to be Ratan Tata.

This is true for every aspect of life. You see an old couple walk hand in hand and think they are lucky to have each other. But what we don't realize is the constant effort that has gone in building that relationship. The innumerable things that came in between, the sacrifices they made keeping the relationship above their own likes and dislikes and as a result, they are what they are today.

You see a man aged about 70 running in the morning. You see his fitness and wish you could also be that fit at that age. But you need to understand that he has been exercising for the past 40 years without break. That means he has never enjoyed the so-called morning sleep which you hold so close to your heart.

You need to be willing to do what it takes to live the life which you aspire for. Just dreaming? Everybody does it. Very few understand the efforts required behind the results. Nothing comes for free. Dreams backed by sincere efforts are sure to give you success. To make your dreams come true, WAKE UP AND START WORKING!

14

Parenting by Example

Ravi, ten years old, wakes up at 5.30 am, brushes his teeth, sit with his books and studies till 7.15 am. Then he polishes his shoes, bathes and dons his uniform, eats his breakfast and cleans his plate, is fully ready five minutes before the van arrives, goes to school, returns in the evening, changes his dress which is still clean, eats a snack, plays for about an hour, finishes his homework, then goes to sleep. Even imagining this ideal child is so boring. Most of us cannot even handle an ideal child. Children are naughty, disobedient and very unpredictable in nature, and that's what makes them children. Otherwise we could be calling them adults, and they would be correcting us.

It is unthinkable that when we advice our children they immediately change according to our instructions. The first time I catch my son telling a lie I have to definitely tell him he is wrong. But if I expect him to always speak only the truth from that instant, I'm wrong. Next time I catch him lying, I need to correct him again. This might happen again and again, so there is no point in getting frustrated. Believe me, it's easier teaching a child than an adult, as the child is willing to adapt and always under the impression that mummy knows best.

In our urge to teach children and make them perfect, we try to influence them too much and almost try everything possible to make them super beings. Is this really required or possible? It's a general practice to say "You are a good boy right? Then finish your dinner." The immediate response of my nephew when he was two years old was, "No, I'm a bad boy," and he'll continue to do what he wanted to do. I always admired this character of him. No pressure to impress others and hence he is free to do whatever he wants to do. Even as adults we are still fighting to overcome other people consciousness. Every child has something very unique which needs to be developed to its full potential. It is our responsibility to lead children to identify and achieve their passion.

True, we need to teach our children every possible thing. But just preaching is not teaching. They learn far better by example. Set an example which your child follows and learns the right actions in the right manner. When we were in a jolly mood enjoying some good music in our car, waiting at a red signal, a lorry behind us was honking continuously. My son immediately said, "Even If you keep honking, my mom won't abide it," with pride in his eyes. By this, I know that he'll never break traffic rules when he grows up as he has associated respecting road rules with a lot of pride.

By giving a lecture on cleanliness we can't teach them cleanliness. The environment in which they grow has to be clean enough all the time so that they will find it difficult to fit in an unclean environment. They will learn only by our example. This could pertain to staying level-headed, daily prayer time, maintaining healthy habits, watching less TV, respecting elders, not wasting food, polite behaviour with staff, not showing off your wealth, avoiding loud behaviour in the house, not entertaining too many friends, reading more books, less internet and mobile phone usage, identifying and avoiding false friends... The list is endless.

Whatever you want to teach your child, lead by example and hold on to this belief that your child is a masterpiece, by which parenting becomes a great joy and pleasure.

15

What is your Binding Factor?

Since six months, Arjun has regularly gone jogging every morning without break. His parents are overjoyed that he has become a health freak. But the fact of the matter is that Arjun saw a pretty girl jogging every morning and wanted an opportunity to be with her, leading to his health freak avatar. I laughed my heart out when Arjun confessed this to me. But I realized that people have hidden or unstated reasons for every action they choose to perform (or not perform).

90% of our lives revolve around the different roles that form our daily routines. We do a lot of routine activities, but are they mechanical or have we ever analyzed why are we performing these tasks? With detailed analysis and honest replies, we may be surprised to recognize our own thought patterns and intentions. In Arjun's case, if the binding factor between him and his action is maintaining his health, he is on the right track. The results and the benefits would be phenomenal. But when the actual reason is something else, which could just be trying to impress the jogging girl, motivation will be low, his jogging won't continue if she stops jogging in his locality, and the results would be average.

People go to work every day. If the invisible binding factor is passion for work, they will be least bothered by low remuneration, additional responsibilities, overtime, etc. Such committed people go to work every day with untiring zest and work becomes their salvation. Over a period of time, if you analyze their results it would be phenomenal. But for people whose binding factor for working is something else like a dependant family, more commitments, not getting a better job, etc., they consistently perform very poorly even after long years of service.

You get married and do your best to impress your spouse. If the invisible binding factor is your mutual love, all other hurdles, shortfalls and relatives' opposition would be just minor problems to be overcome and the marriage will flourish. Over a period of time you will then be lauded as the role model couple. But if the binding factor is something else, like security, getting married with no choice, money, status, etc., life becomes too painful even without other hurdles. Every challenge becomes a thorny issue and you just pull on.

You do everything for your children. Your only aim is to provide them nothing but the best. If the binding factor is just love, their actions, words, disobedience... nothing would be a problem. You joyfully sail along with them in their life, guiding them all the time. But if the binding factor is something else like wanting to feel proud of their results, somebody to take care of you in your old age, etc., then you'll find life very strenuous, and disappointment is certain.

You need not answer anybody, but be honest with yourself. Avoid doing anything where you think your binding factor is not right. It's better not to do something rather than to drag along with no results.

Desired results are possible only when your actions have the right binding factor. For 90% of our actions we don't even analyze why we are doing them. Start asking "Why am I doing this?" for every action. If you are convinced your binding factor is not for selfish reasons, then go ahead and do what you are doing, else pause and ask yourself, "What will happen if I don't do this?" Everything will fall in place and for the first time you'll feel that you are the author of your life.

16

Endorsement

It's always fun spending time with children. We feel so cleansed by seeing their innocence. If you observe them closely, you can see that whenever you give them the attention they desire, they try to impress you more by sharing something they have done or learnt. It could be a painting, a rhyme or a story, or something where you have no choice but to tell them GOOOOOOOD, which is an endorsement they expect from the world. Children grow. But they never grow out of this desire to be endorsed by the outside world.

We don't mind giving such endorsements to children. For every small action we appreciate them so much. "You finished all the food! Good boy," "You danced so well – Sooppeeer," "You coloured this! Oh beautiful," etc. But as they grow, the world almost stops giving such endorsements. In order to be appreciated and complimented, a person has to prove he is academically brilliant, or very good in some extracurricular activity, or is earning beyond comprehension, or has achieved something truly great. As a result, most of the time, he keeps seeking ways to get such appreciation, which is the root cause of many unwanted thoughts and actions.

Pick up a conversation with total strangers and they are eager to share their achievements, actual or imagined. The desire to blow one's trumpet and expecting the world to endorse our greatness is a huge burden most of us carry. This is most seen in organizations where everybody wants to take credit for any and all positive achievements (and obviously, not for failures). "See, I told you," is a commonly heard statement.

People go to impossible lengths for getting such endorsements. In most cases, doing is not a problem, but the seeking of recognition creates problems. When a painter starts thinking, "Will the world accept this concept?" even before trying to paint, he'll never be able to create a masterpiece. Similarly, without focusing on what we can do, if we keep thinking about recognition all the time, it becomes difficult to bring out the best in us.

A mother was trying to feed her child while he was totally engrossed with painting and was least interested to eat. When his mother said, "You are a good boy right? Then finish dinner fast," he immediately retorted, "No I'm a bad boy" and continued to paint. Now the child is not bothered if his mother thinks he is good or bad. The mother has no choice but to allow her son to do whatever he wants. By ignoring his mother's endorsement, the child has full freedom to do whatever he wants. Similarly if we can just drop the urge to crave for endorsements from the world outside, we have full freedom to do whatever we want.

What we need is an endorsement from inside. Your inner voice should say: "Yes! This is what I want to do." Listen to your inner voice. If it says 'Yes,' feel proud about yourself. If it says 'No,', pause and correct yourself. But keep doing, keep doing and keep on doing. Don't pause to check if you are getting recognition. Nothing in the world can stop what you truly deserve. Trust yourself and march ahead. The world will definitely pave a way for the resolute soul.

17

Existential Aloneness

The sound of rain always brings me joy. Listening to it with closed eyes in the warmth of a cosy bed in a cold room early in the morning is almost meditative. I just half opened my eyes to see if my son was sleeping and realized that he had already woken up to study. Not wanting to miss out on the experience of enjoying the sound, I lay there motionless, trying to visualize the rain outside. The child in me started playing in the rain, of course in my mind, but was interrupted by my inner voice: "You are all alone in this experience."

Realizing that I could not afford to be late, I reluctantly left the bed. Mornings are usually very busy: instructions to the maid, breakfast, lunch, etc. When I dropped my son at school on time, I breathed a sigh of relief. Driving to my office, I switched on the music and started enjoying it. As I forgot myself in the music, the voice interrupted, "You are all alone in this experience."

When I stepped into office, my colleagues had already arrived. I greeted them, sat with a friend for a quick chat, checked my to-do list and plunged into my job. Generally, I forget myself while creating a scheme design. It feels as if I'm inside the computer, building the scheme brick by brick. I started a scheme design for a new project at Vellore. Sensing that something was not okay with the design, I kept working on it, but my heart never said WOW, so I decided to take a small break. I just closed my eyes and sat back in my chair, in my own world, when my inner voice repeated: "You are all alone in this experience."

After a hectic day, I went home and was greeted by my son. Oh we really enjoy chatting with each other at the end of the day. He wanted some clarifications in Biology. I was too tired, but I never postpone anything related to his studies. So I sat with him and explained the topic. We had dinner; when I hit the bed I was too exhausted. I took a book and started reading from where I had left off. As I drowned in the book the familiar voice said, "You are all alone in this experience."

My mind started pondering on this repeated statement. In our journey of life, we have our roles to play, our responsibilities that need to be fulfilled. We have people around us all the time. But somewhere in our lives we are all alone. That's a fact. In our happiness we are all alone. In our fear we are all alone. In our crying we are all alone. In our emotions we are all alone. I now understood "Existential Aloneness" which my teacher had explained.

Any child is born in this world with some purpose. From the minute when the umbilical cord is cut, a child starts living its life. The fact is that till death the child faces its life alone. We could be surrounded by parents, relatives, friends and what not. But the fact is that we have to face life alone. There is a spiritual loneliness in every soul. If we can understand this, our crying could be handled with much greater maturity and inner peace. On realizing this, I went down on my knees to talk to my Lord: "God, you have sent me with a purpose which I'm not aware of. Just teach me to have faith in You and walk this life without fear, holding your hand," and I could feel the smile of the inner voice.

18

The Three Relationships

I really enjoy listening to my teacher as he discusses even the most complicated subjects in very simple form, in a way I can understand. Somehow anything looks easy when he explains. The other day he was discussing relationships. As usual, I started thinking what I should implement. In a nutshell, he said we should work on three relationships:

My relationship With myself

My relationship With others

My relationship With my God

My Relationship with Myself:

I thought I could implement this easily as the only factor available here is me. I just need to love myself for what I am. I can just set targets in every role I play. I can start with small achievable goals, achieve them and keep rising in my own eyes. I can keep raising the bar every time I achieve something and keep patting myself for every milestone achieved. It is just a decision I have to take and I have entire control of this decision. So I concluded, "Oh! This is easy to implement."

My Relationship with My God:

For anything good that happens, we say thanks to God. When something negative happens, we say "God is testing me," "He is giving me an experience to learn," "He is moulding me for something," etc. Always passing on the benefit of doubt to God, we believe that everything would end beautifully. Ultimately, my relationship with my God doesn't suffer at any point of time. So again I concluded, "Oh! This is easy to implement."

My Relationship with OTHERS:

The entire drama in relationship begins with this. The minute we see a person, we start a process. We start judging them, though we don't know anything about that person. Then we do everything to build that relationship. Oh! we stay an angel of a person as long as we are not sure whether the other also feels the same way. But once we get a glimpse of comfort, we reduce the gap slowly. Without our knowledge we keep expanding something called "Expectation". When there is permanence in that relationship then this "Expectation" becomes too difficult to handle. The more you love a person, the more hurt you get because you expect them to reciprocate love in a way you understand love which becomes too suffocating over a period of time. Even with strangers, if they don't behave the way you expect them to behave, you get so worked up.

Then I realized that somebody else other than me, their actions, deeds, thoughts on which I have no control, are involved in this which makes the whole thing so complicated. But I have absolute control on my

"Expectation". This also plays an equal part in complicating the whole thing. I can work on controlling my expectations, which can protect me from any hurt. So I concluded, "Oh! This is not easy to implement, but I can start from where I can start."

19

Today is the day!

I was finally brave enough to ask myself, "What are all the things which you wish to do personally for yourself?" We generally avoid this question as we are scared to face the answer. I created a list of things which I always wanted to do, but have only postponed. The list is surprisingly long, though it covers a lot of minor matters which are postponed or forgotten, but never done. My concern is not on the major goals, as I'm very confident that I am constantly working in that direction. But my concern is on the huge list of small things in the list.

The list included: 'Visit to this designer shop one day,' 'Try tennis with my son,' 'Go swimming at least weekly,' 'Try speaking in Hindi,' 'Create a Facebook account and see how many friends I can trace,' 'Lie down in my mother's lap and watch a movie,' 'Try baking one day,' etc. Why was I neglecting these simple things for so long? I had no idea. As I pondered about it, I knew these jobs were desirable and doable, but remained unsure if I would ever make efforts to complete them.

Desire drives us. I'm happy that I have a big to-do list, which tells me that I still have the zest to live. But my concern is: When will I do what I want to do? What am I waiting for? Is there an action plan? I know if I don't have an action plan for these personal matters, they may always remain unticked in the wish list. A simple solution would be to write down a date against every item, possibly one item per month. But until you fix a date against it, be assured it will never get done.

But just assigning dates will not lead to the jobs' completion on schedule, meaning you have to fulfil your promises by those dates. In addition, this list will never be closed. The more personal dreams you fulfill, the more you will discover new personal goals to reach. After finally visiting the designer shop in the list, you'll see yet another new showroom which you would want to visit. So the list is endless and always changing. The best part of implementation is that at any given point of time, the list you hold is constantly updated and fresh.

Assigning a date against every item, following an action plan and completing the jobs one at a time would automatically become part of your habit. Then it will hold good even for your ambitious goals as attitude does not care where you shape them it gets shaped. Fulfilling and updating your wish list, small or big, will become a lifestyle and you will be surprised to see the way you start living a holistic life. So, why are you waiting? Grab a paper and a pen and get the list in place. Life is so beautiful. You can't afford to miss anything.

20

A complete Women

It was one of those days when I wanted some me-time. I was reading a magazine in the warmth of my bed when a picture caught my eye. I saw a very prominent lady posing with her head on her son's shoulder, saying, "Yeah! He has grown," with pride in her eyes. I personally know how much this genius has accomplished in her life. Yet the pride in her eyes as she was resting her head on her son's shoulder was unparalleled.

Analyzing the other pictures in that magazine, I saw various pictures of women known to be great and successful in their fields. In the pictures where they posed with a close friend or family member—spouse, child, father—the ladies were holding their hands and beaming with inner joy. I realized that this smile, this self-satisfaction, is not for their career success, but for the peace they experienced in the company of their loved ones. This is the very nature of women and there is nothing that puts her down because of this nature. A successful actress quits her profession without a second thought when she gets married, confident that the happiness and fulfilment she will get in the warmth of a family will be far greater than what was achieved in the limelight.

Women instinctively enjoy taking care of people whom they love. That is the reason we admire and salute mothers, because there is no match to their love and affection. We all know how women willingly make huge sacrifices to support the lives of their loved ones. While this is a quality to be admired, we should also understand that this very quality hampers their personal and career growth, in turn decelerating national economic growth. The myriad talents of almost half the population (females solely in domestic roles) are mostly under-utilized. Better or optimal utilization of this untapped ocean of talent will lead to phenomenal growth in all fields, and we will be on the fast track to becoming a super power.

How can we empower the women in our proximity to start earning (or start earning more)? Yes, give them the family support without which they may crumble, but also push them to showcase their various talents, support them by discussing possible fields of work. Motivate them by saying that by becoming financially independent they can give a better life to their children, which should prod them into action. Identify nearby self help groups and see if you can make them join up. A lot can be done even sitting at home as Internet has literally shrunk the world to your lap. If she shows signs of financial prudence, introduce her to share trading or other trading activity.

A lot can be done and needs to be done. There is a huge demand for shrewd man power and there is also a huge untapped talent pool available, mostly females. Let us play our roles in bridging the gap between the two. We'll definitely celebrate womanhood, but let us also give life to their dreams and enable them to live a complete live.

21

The Hidden Agenda

Truly thrilled when I was offered a job in campus interview, I joined the organization immediately after graduation as a trainee engineer along with another girl. We reported to a manager, who was a very sweet person. We underwent some orientation and training courses, and life was fun.

Allotted our roles, I was assigned to report to a tough senior (who did not report to my manager) and he was least helpful or encouraging. He refused to teach me anything or to assign any job, expecting me to learn everything on my own. I felt that the other girl was far luckier as she still reported to our manager and breezed through office work with clear instructions and lighter work loads.

My life became a nightmare. I tried talking to my senior, but he did not respond. Beyond a point, when I could bear it no more, I went and explained matters to my manager and asked for a change of department, but she refused. Instead, she tried building my relationship with my senior by sending us to trainings together, asking us to organize trips together, etc. and I hated every bit of it. I wondered why my manager disliked me.

Thrown into the ocean of office work, I had no choice but to learn swimming. I started creating lists and flow charts to understand what was happening in the department. I would open the source code to understand its functionality. Then I documented the entire project, created a step-by-step manual, and gave it to the operators. I automated five systems which were earlier manual. It took me a full year to get a hold on the system.

When my senior suddenly fell sick, I had to complete the monthly financial closing. My heart was palpitating as we began the procedure, which was usually completed by midnight. But all my hard work had paid off; the job was completed by 7 pm. When I reported this to my manager, she was pleasantly surprised. She called me for a coffee to her cabin and said, "I knew you were tough and could make it. That is why I assigned that department to you." This statement shocked me, because all along, I had thought she didn't like me. Only now did I understand that she believed in me and was working for my well-being.

A few days later my senior said, "I'm happy for you. I could never come out of the day-to-day activities in the department and I never wanted you to be caught in the same routine. Now you are actually analyzing and computerizing, which is what is expected of you. Only now did I understand that he also had always been my well-wisher. I realized that I never had the complete picture of what was happening. I saw the immediate things on my table and cried foul. I blamed everything and everybody for whatever I went through without a second thought.

Suddenly I realized I had been cribbing all through without realizing that I was the chosen one.

From then on, whenever I face tough times, I tell myself, "I still don't know the big picture. Just hold on, maybe there is something which I'm not seeing." I have experienced that challenging times often turn out to be the most important turning points in my life. My teacher always says, "God upsets your plans to execute his plans and his plans are the best for you." If we can just hold on to this belief, NOTHING in this world can stop us.

22

I WANT WHAT I WANT

Anandhi was excited as they were planning to go out that evening. Her husband had promised to come a little early and take them out for dinner. She always wished if she could go out alone with her husband and daughter. But the in-laws being at home, it had always been a dream. Her husband arrived early as promised. She wanted to wear jeans but didn't, thinking her in-laws would disapprove. Though it was not to her taste, she chose the red churidar kurta which her husband had gifted her, thinking he would like it.

When they got ready, her mother-in-law said, "We are tired. You go without us." For a second she felt very relieved. But she said, "No ma. We'll go to some place nearby. You please come," knowing that unless she said these words, the in-laws would mistake her. As they were leaving, her daughter said, "We'll go to an Italian restaurant." Everybody liked Italian, except Anandhi. Yet she said, "Anything is fine." After dinner, she wanted to go window shopping in the mall, but her father-in-law said, "Oh! I'm tired," and her husband decided to go home.

When she hit the bed she felt very upset but had no clue why. She had gone out for dinner and spent time with her family, which was always welcome, but still she felt sad and unsatisfied. Tears started trickling down. Her husband yelled: "Just because you couldn't do window shopping you'll cry and make me feel sick. Whatever I do, you won't feel happy. You don't think about others' comfort. You want what you want," and slammed the door. She felt even worse and very lonely.

Whenever you try to be somebody other than your natural self, you often end up achieving nothing. A mask doesn't help much. Right from our growing years, we are told to share our things, listen to elders, don't talk against them, etc. and we become conditioned to think that if we express ourselves, people will mistake us. We have been trained to just listen and do what others expect of us. When you do things which you don't want to do, there is a split inside and you end up feeling, "Nobody understands me." You'll feel frustrated and very lonely at times.

First, we need to understand that nobody is perfect and wanting to please everybody will not work. This doesn't mean that you can be arrogant and live selfishly. You have to adjust and accommodate for your near and dear ones. It is your duty to take care of your loved ones. But at the same time, doing what you want to do is not a crime. You want to go out alone with your husband? Tell everybody you are going on a date. Wear the outfits you like. Go to a restaurant of your choice, spend time and enjoy. Nobody will have a problem with this approach as long as you take care of their needs also.

Stop thinking what others will think for every action of yours. You can never keep the world happy by being what they want you to be. Do something only when it makes you happy; also find happiness in making your family members and colleagues happy. Do what your heart says. You want to work, learn something, wear that dress to see him smile, go to the parlour, cook Italian for your daughter, say "Love you" – just do it the way you want. With love and happiness from within, you'll see the world getting attracted towards you and you would have missed nothing to earn that world. Tell yourself and the world around you: "YES - I want what I want."

23

Expand your world

On Women's day, I made plans to meet an old friend who is a homemaker. Her son is employed and her husband is generally very silent. While waiting for her, I felt sorry for her, thinking she must be very lonely and bored. When she arrived, I couldn't take my eyes off her. Full of life, she wished me "Happy Women's Day."

She had a lunch party, a dinner party invitation for Women's day and her phone kept ringing with greetings for Women's day. She was on her way to a hospital to visit a friend and I was zapped with her energy as she moved around. She was involved in so many activities that I actually realized I would have to take an appointment if I wanted to spend some time with her.

I was amazed at the way she had built a world around her. She was into gym, yoga, small time retailer, beautician, pilgrimage tour guide and her cooking is so famous that she usually cooks for minimum six to seven people as she always has some guests. For a very long time after she left, I could feel the vibrations she had left behind.

Without any speeches she taught me: "Our life is what we decide it to be." I have seen a lot of women settle so very easily into the role of wife, mother, daughter-in-law, that after a few years, we can't even correlate them with their past avatars. When we observe a group of girls in college, we hear loud bursts of laughter, their dress sense, their radiant smiles, the talents they display in different competitions, the way they study, the way they walk as if the whole world has been created just to serve them. But where do these girls go after marriage? Lost? Is it a loss to them or to the world or is it mutual?

I have seen very talented and artistic girls working in MNCs, girls who make a difference in their organization, then just quit their careers as soon as they get married. They tell themselves they will resume work when the children grow up; meantime, they are full time occupied with serving the family. A lady immerses herself happily into her family without anybody asking for it.

Now as long as everything goes perfectly well, she doesn't feel the pinch of it. But if something goes wrong in her small world, everything comes to a standstill. When she turns around seeking help, she realizes she has lost everybody other than her immediate family in the process and now has nobody to turn too. Don't ever shrink your world for anybody's sake. Take family as an additional responsibility in your existing life.

Anything is possible only when you consider it possible. It is possible to integrate your existing world into your married life. People will come and go from your life, but this should never shake your world. Expand your world so that any action of anybody in your world doesn't shake you up completely. This is a caution to all women. Think twice before you shrink your world. For your own selfish reason, keep expanding your world. Explore new possibilities and keep yourself so busy that you no longer have time for the petty things which bother you today. We live in a beautiful world. Don't miss it for any reason and let the world not miss you.

24

Face It

Vineet's heart skipped a beat on receiving a phone call from his son Sudar's class teacher. She said that she had been wanting to meet him since two months, but Sudar had always said that Vineet was not available. So she had called him directly to ask when they could meet. Vineet met her the same day. It was a casual initiative by the teacher to be in touch with her student's parents. She gave her feedback on Sudar's performance and where they need to focus. He thanked her for her interest in his son's studies. . On reaching home, he confronted Sudar, who bowed his head and mumbled, "I was scared that she would complain about something. Also, I thought she would forget after some time, so you will never come to know about it." Not sure how to respond, Vineet just said, "Don't repeat it."

He sat at the dining table with a confused mind. His wife Neeta was discussing the upcoming festival and the shopping they needed to do for their parents. When Vineet said, "We'll use your savings for this festival.

I'll pay you after my bonus comes," Neeta's face turned pale. Asked why she was upset, she said: "I used those savings for some personal expenditure for my sister. You never ask for my savings, so I thought you'll never come to know about it." Vineet remained silent, because she had full freedom to do what she wanted, he could not fathom why she should hide such matters from him.

Feeling very upset, he went to bed and fell asleep immediately. Next day, he tried to put the earlier day's unpleasant feelings behind him and left for office, trying to be cheerful. At office, he checked his mails and prepared the to-do list. His boss arrived and Vineet could sense that his boss was fuming.

"You said you have replied to that customer mail yesterday when I checked. But late last night the customer made a huge issue of no response from our side. Don't give me a wrong status any day," and he left. Vineet suddenly remembered that he just told his boss that he had sent the mail, to cover up for the moment and was planning to send it subsequently. But in his confusion, he had completely forgotten about it. Suddenly he could decipher the domestic events of the previous day.

Whenever we face a difficult situation, we only think how to manage for the moment. We don't mind doing or saying anything just to escape from that situation, not realizing that we will have to face it one day. Without analyzing if it is right or not, as long as we can delay facing it, we think we have outsmarted everybody. The more we delay facing it, the more it actually balloons. Avoiding a difficult situation or keeping silent about it will only kill us eventually.

What we need to understand is that any problem has a solution, and there is a right way to solve it. Sometimes it can be a tough situation. Manipulating the events, hiding ourselves, being silent is not going to help in any manner. We'll fall in our own eyes. Facing it is the only solution. People who love us truly will accept us as we are with our flaws as long as we are willing to correct ourselves. That is why a mother can always forgive her children irrespective of their flaws. Just have confidence in yourself and face any situation. Do only what you think is right. You will grow in your own eyes as well as in others' eyes.

25

Huge Responsibility

Entering my cabin, I saw some cheques waiting to be signed. I verified the bills and clarified some points before I signed them. Recalling the days when I started my career, I used to think my manager's job was the easiest, with people around to do all the work. I used to feel jealous when I saw her sign approvals and cheques, the respect she got when she walked past.

But today, when I sign the cheques, I appreciate the kind of pressure a manager or owner has. It is just not signing; understanding what you are signing and why, is a huge responsibility. Every paper has to be checked and understood before signing. By your signature you actually authorize people to go ahead, hence the responsibility is shifted to your shoulders.

As we grow, we start accepting more responsibilities. A promotion makes us very happy, because we know the position and the perks it promises. Seeing our boss commanding and getting work done, his respect, etc., we feel excited about the promotion. But do we really see the pressures he handles? When we actually get into the role and execute it, we start complaining that there is too much work to do.

A promotion has to be understood in terms of the responsibility it brings rather than perks or position. We should acknowledge each promotion as an additional responsibility in addition to what we are doing right now. In fact, if you think you are not ready for the additional responsibility for lack of skills or personal commitments, it is better not to accept the promotion, rather than accepting it and then succumbing under pressure.

Every success is a responsibility. If you are number 1 in any sport, every time you play you have the huge responsibility to live up to the standard which you have created for yourself. If you are an artist, you have to outperform yourself and live up to the expectations of your fans. If you are a politician, you have to sacrifice your personal interests for the sake of public who trusted you for their welfare. Becoming popular is never a status but a responsibility.

Even in our personal lives, everything should be seen as a responsibility. As students we are responsible for the output we produce. Taking responsibility for each and every single drop of sweat our parents and teachers shed for our sake, we should achieve the best results and show them that you respect their effort. When you get married, beyond all the fun and fancies of marriage, you have the huge responsibility of mingling the other's life with yours with a commitment to be there till the end. On becoming a parent, beyond the joy experienced is the huge responsibility that you'll do everything in your capacity to ensure a good life for the newborn. Student, son, spouse, parent, etc. is never a status but a responsibility.

In every role, you are expected to do your part. No elevation or promotion is a title assigned or a status given. You are expected to behave suitably and responsibly. Ask yourself: What more should I do? What else should I take up? Become a responsible individual. Be accountable to every role which you are given. Take up more responsibilities without asking: What will I get? Life will become more meaningful and complete.

26

De-stress Yourself

My son and I were packing for his stay at hostel. We prepared the to-do list and did a lot of shopping. Two months just flew past in the preparation. When the D-day came, I couldn't believe that I actually had to leave him and return alone to a house that looked deserted and empty. I was cursing myself for my decision. I have never felt so lonely before and didn't feel like doing anything.

As days passed, I realized I had to accept the facts and keep going. First, I accepted that I needed to immerse myself in activities to distract me from my son's absence. Deciding to work on distracting my mind, I hit upon various activities which could keep me occupied. No. I'm not talking about meditation or yoga.

I grabbed a few books – crime novels, management books and spiritual books – then spent a lot of time with them for a few days. When we are gloomy, we just have to avoid thinking anything for that matter and dissolving in books helped to achieve it. For me, it was books, but it could be anything that distracts you by keeping you occupied. Music, TV, painting, writing, art work, cooking, puzzles or even computer games for that matter – it could be anything. Just don't allow your mind to be idle. Force your mind into things which you like and force yourself to do it.

Then I just took a break to visit old friends. A change in the environment helps to eliminate your pain faster. New surroundings, new people, exploring new places definitely helps you to forget painful thoughts and gives a direction to your thinking. No medicine in the world can match laughter. When friends chat together, we have no idea why we burst out laughing. We laughed and laughed till there were tears in our eyes. Laughter makes your heart feel light and free. Take an initiative to arrange for such a tour or a get together and laugh your heart out.

Try things you have never done before. When I joined tennis class, the coach gave me a confused look. I told her with a smile that I was not looking at playing in tournaments but just wanted to learn. Learning something new keeps your heart young and makes you more enthusiastic. Learn something new, something you have missed in the past. Swimming, skating, music, dance, language, crafts – anything new which you always wanted to learn, but never had an opportunity. Age is never a barrier to learn anything.

Many of us are under stress or depression. Loss of a loved one, issues relating to health, monetary matters, parenting, peer pressure – it could be anything that pulls down our spirits. Sometimes we feel there is nobody to understand, help or support us. But no help is bigger than self help. We don't need medicine or a psychiatrist to help us during this time. Even if we take medical or psychiatric help, our personal effort is the all-important essential catalyst needed.

We need to take control of our life.

Life will always be a mix of both good and not so good things. We can avoid stress and depression in our lives only when we take control of our mind and steer it in a positive direction, especially during bad times. True, sometimes the pain is too much to bare. But believe me, it is just a passing phase of life and something better is in store, so you can be sure that the best is yet to come. Just follow any technique which helps you to hold on till you see the good timess again.

27

Tired – A Mirage

Holidaying with a group is always fun. After quite a long time, we planned an office get together, a three day trip. The staff were charged with energy right from the start of the week. Planning and organizing is always fun. Travel, food, stay, sightseeing, games, music, etc. were planned and organized. Teams were created and given different responsibilities. It's always a good feeling to watch people from different departments come together for a common cause and work together. The main agenda for a trip is only to bring people together, so that it reflects in their work.

After a long journey on the first day, we reached the resort. I thought my staff would be tired and might want to rest. Rooms were allotted and they were told that coffee would be served at the lawn in the evening. Checking into my room, I unpacked and freshened up. I was almost certain that everybody would be resting. I couldn't sleep and the scene around the resort was so beautiful that I decided to explore the place. On reaching an open space in the resort, I saw some of our people playing cricket. I sat there watching them play and slowly the entire staff had assembled there. Then we split into teams and started playing various games before going for dinner. The fun continued till late in the night.

Next day we planned to see a waterfall which entailed about two hours of mountain climbing. Some lady staff were caught unaware but did not back out. It was fun climbing and seeing the waterfall was once-in-a-lifetime experience. We agreed that this was a sight not to be missed. The return journey downhill was more challenging, especially for those with unsuitable footwear, but we managed because there was no choice.

I thought they would retire for the rest of the day as they were complaining about leg pain. But when we reached the resort, the fun started again and continued till midnight. Next day we had planned trekking, and I was very sure that half of them would back out. But when we assembled in the morning, I was pleasantly surprised to see the entire team present. The team kept surprising me with the energy they had till the end.

While returning, I realized that tiredness is just a mindset. The body may become tired, but the mind never tires as long as it feels positive and happy. With the power to pull the body back, the mind overcomes physical fatigue to a great extent. We have seen motivated people working long hours with perseverance, treating every setback as a challenge and delivering great results. Such human dynamos continue to work in their field even after they retire. We have also seen less motivated people unable to focus and always claiming to be tired or sick, with consistently poor performances

So whenever I feel tired, it only means I'm doing things where the mind is not feeling either positive or happy. That is a signal which tells me to stop and check out the action that is the cause for the drain in energy. Anything we do has to make us happy doing it. At the end of the day, if we can hit the bed still energetic and enthusiastic, then we can be sure there is no split anywhere in our day to day routine. If we fill our life with actions which only makes us happy, we can delete the word "tired" out of our life.

if you still feel tired physically, just tell yourself that this is the last day of the trip and gear up for a new experience. Reassure yourself that something interesting and exciting is awaiting, then see how you get recharged. Let our energy be our identity. Let's live life with zest and enthusiasm.

28

GRAND PARENTING

Parenting is a very beautiful aspect of our lives. And before you realize it, your child has grown up and is talking about politics, life, technology, etc. Sometimes children even declare that you don't know anything in life. We think parenting is a lifetime relationship and are lethargic or complacent about it. But it is a constantly changing equation. In the initial years, your children are completely yours. But as they start exploring the world, they slowly build a life of their own. You become a part of their life, but not the centre. In today's scenario, where both parents are working, the children are with grandparents most of the time. Parents often miss out on a lot of things with their child as they don't find time. In fact, some schools now celebrate grandparents' day.

Children always love to be pampered and grandparents are usually happy to do so, taking care of the grandchildren as long as they do not have any other commitments. After a hectic day at office, parents can't handle the children with sufficient patience, so obviously the children become closer to grandparents. They want grandparents to feed them, do homework with them, play with them and even sleep with them. This has both advantages and disadvantages. With your parents taking care of your children, your offspring would not be deprived of love and affection. Hence they would grow with emotional stability. But are grandparents adequately equipped to build grandchildren's personality for today's requirements? That is a big question.

Grandparents must understand that the way they parented their own children will not work today with grandchildren. They also must realize that pampering a child beyond a certain level is least desirable. Also, they shouldn't take complete responsibility for the child. Leave complete responsibility to the parents and give them a chance to be parents. If the parents are working, take care of the children when they are away for work. But beyond that, please avoid interfering between children and their parents. This would help the child in the long run. The more children find a friend in the parent, the more likely they are to share their personal lives and seek advice. And this is the magic wand for parents to have an influence in their children's lives. Only when the child sees a friend in you, will he confide in you and listen to your advice.

Parenting is an art. Your relationship with your child is more than just biological and instinctive; it needs to be constantly groomed and strengthened. To teach them moral values, you need to play with them, tell suitable stories with embedded moral messages for these values to be etched in their systems. You can't start giving them lectures on moral values when they are adults. To teach etiquette, you need to display it yourself and the child has to watch it again and again to learn. Each child is unique in its own right. Parents need to uncover their children's latent talents and encourage them to build and develop these talents. Grooming them in every aspect of life is a huge task which can't be delegated to somebody else.

There is so much to enjoy seeing your children grow. Every minute is precious and you are not going to get it again with the child. Enjoy parenting. Build the roots of your relationship so strong that it takes care of the child's life even when you are no longer with them physically.

29

Tooo much

Diwali is always fun. Granny feels blessed to do Lakshmi pooja, mom tries a lot of things at kitchen, dad keeps checks on the budget, cousins get together for a lot of laughter and the children can't bat an eyelid from the crackers. There is always an air of excitement about Diwali.

Last Diwali the kids were bursting crackers as my brother was policing them. They never get tired of crackers and after a couple of hours my brother was losing patience. We were chatting about how it was when we were young.

Diwali in those days

We bought one set of new clothes each for Diwali. Hectic shuttling between home and the tailor's shop was the norm, and we would be nervous that our garments wouldn't be ready for Diwali. Brimming with joy, we would take our clothes from the tailor and keenly anticipate for

Diwali to arrive so that we could wear the new dress. Dad would buy the crackers just a few days before Diwali. We would check these items and if something had been missed, we would start negotiating to see if we could buy that also.

We would start bursting the small crackers two days before, after promising not to touch the rest of the crackers. One day before Diwali, mom would start making sweets and we would shuttle between kitchen and our room to see if we could sneak something out of the kitchen. Mom would be very strict and say we could eat these only after pooja. Waiting for the new dress, sweets and crackers, for cousins to arrive would all be so pleasant.

After so much waiting, we could never be able to sleep the previous night. We would wake up early in the morning, take oil bath, wear new dress and burst crackers while it was still dark. As there were many people at home, each of us would get personal quotas of crackers and sweets, which we always felt inadequate. At the end of Diwali, we would be eagerly anticipating the next Diwali already.

Diwali now

Nowadays, we buy readymade outfits for Diwali with no need of chasing tailors. Even otherwise, we already have new dresses, so buying Diwali dresses is not thrilling; it is just a custom to be observed. Some food items may be made at home for pooja. Other sweets and savouries are mostly bought, and are available all though the year, so they are not very tantalizing.

We buy crackers as soon as they are available and start bursting them from day one, without waiting for the festival. Cousins visit us for just an hour to wish us. On Diwali day, getting up early seems meaningless as we have the whole day free. As we are going to be at home, we don't feel like wearing the new dress, except maybe during pooja, then immediately change to comfortable clothing after that. We have good TV programmes which nobody wants to miss. True, it's good to be at home with family, lazing around, munching, watching TV and of course pooja. But beyond that, do we really eagerly anticipate the next Diwali? Hardly.

Diwali celebrations nowadays have left me with this lingering thought:

1. When I have too much of something, I no longer long for it. I don't cherish it, as I did when I had less of it. I feel grateful that that I no longer cherish many of the things I craved as a child since I have them in such plenty as to be satiated.

2. I also need to be grateful for the things which I don't have in plenty yet, as they give me targets which I can chase and there is so much joy in searching, waiting and working towards achieving them.

30

ASK

When I was visiting my friend after a long time, her daughter came running to greet me. When we see kids, we realize we are getting old and it brought a smile to my face. The child happily took the box of chocolates I had brought for her. My friend took the box from her, gave her one chocolate to eat and kept the box on the table. Meeting after a very long time, we had so much to catch up on. So we settled down with coffee and snacks. We had so much to talk about and time just whizzed away.

At regular frequency the child would come and ask for one more chocolate and my friend would decline. The child neither insisted nor cried for chocolates. She would just say "No. Ok," and leave. But she would return after some time with the same request. After five or six requests, my friend would laugh and give her a chocolate. I felt that the whole interaction was very cute.

The child never gave up, nor did she cry when rejected. She kept doing what had to be done from her side to get what she wanted, and there was a lot of peace in the whole process. The determination with which she tried again and again, the grace with which she faced rejection, and the peace with which she handled the whole matter was a sight to appreciate. Most importantly, she never stopped asking since mom was constantly refusing, and might refuse again.

Many times, we start thinking on behalf of others and think our idea or request will be rejected. While waiting for the appraisal results, very confident of promotion, one is disappointed on not getting promoted. In such situations, we may usually get angry and depressed, feeling that everybody is against us. We vent these feelings to all our colleagues and friends. But will this solve our problem?

We are reluctant to ask our boss "What happened?" .While approaching our boss, we often think, "Should I ask him? What would be his response? What if he starts yelling at me? What if he gives a list of negative things like you didn't do this, that etc.?" Most of us often remain silent, fearing rejection; as a result, we lose interest in the job. We also tell everybody, "Whatever you do, your inputs are not going to be recognized. So why work?"

Why should we reject ourselves is the big question? If you didn't get the expected promotion, just go and discuss it with your boss right away. Explain your stand; most importantly, analyze his way of judgement and see where the gap is. That will lead to progress. Whatever the outcome of the meeting, we still need to handle it, fix our next target and move on with peace. But it is also possible that you would be given what you wanted because you asked. You never know.

ASK is the magic word. You never know how the other person may react. You lose nothing by asking for what you want, as long as you are able to support it with logic. Handling your request is other person's problem, not yours. Even an infant understands that it has to cry to be fed. The British term is "The squeaky wheel gets the grease." Never be afraid to put forth your ideas, your thoughts or your views on anything, but do it politely. Until you say what you want, there is no way others will come to know about it. Don't reject yourself and crumble inside. Ask and ye shall receive, said Christ. There is only one life. Don't reject yourself and miss out on your life. Live the way you want your life to be, and never give up.

31

Just LOVE

A novel I was reading had the following scene which revealed a new dimension to love.

Hero: You know how much I love you?

Heroine: But James, this is not going to work out. I would be leaving very shortly as my visa is lapsing.

Hero: So what? I never said you should love me or live with me and get stuck here. When we love our children, we don't even know what we mean to them. We can mean anything to them, but our love for them is true. That's how I want it to be between us. This is what I feel for you and I'm expressing it. You are free to do what you want, live where you want. But any day you want to feel loved, I'm just a call away.

My heart missed a beat as I read this. No doubt we love our children, but do they love us back? That is something we take for granted. In any relationship, we perceive something and live. Most of the time, we are not even aware if our perceptions are true. We feel so close to a person and do everything in our capacity to express our love. In the whole process, we miss one thing: Does the other also reciprocate our feelings, actions and sacrifices? Does he or she love you to the extent you love them?

As this can never be explained or measured, it is conveniently ignored; most of the time, it is taken for granted. He is my husband and he has to love me and that is all to it. She is my wife and she has to accept whatever I do and live the life which I ask her to live. Period. When we don't see our love reciprocated, in the way we expect, we get into a cycle of depression. The more dejected we get, the more we start demanding love and attention, which ultimately corrodes the entire relationship.

I met an old and very special friend who used to call me "Bond" as he always believed that we shared a special existential bond. When we met after many years, I could see he still carried the same feeling. He remembered every small incident that took place when we worked together. I could feel that he still believed in the bond between us. But did I take the effort to keep all those memories alive? What he means to me and what I mean to him today are very different and we express it differently. To him, I am still his special 'bond', but to me he is one more friend from my past and this shows when we communicate. Can he handle it when he realizes the difference is the big question?

Say "I love you" and learn to stop with that. We need a large heart to say, "I love you for various reasons I only know, and I don't expect you to do anything about my feeling." My teacher always said "What you do or what you do not do, does not alter my love for you." Ideally, we should implement this with every relationship. To begin with, let us try to "just love" at least the people who really matter to us and expect nothing in return.

32

The Inner War

When the alarm woke me early in the morning for my aerobics session, I could feel the irritation in my eyes. It is true bliss just to lie down in the cosy bed with the air conditioner at 18 degree.

My mind: It is so nice. Bunk aerobics today and catch up from tomorrow. After all, it was a hectic day yesterday and you definitely owe it to your body.

I just ignored temptation and got up from the bed. With track suit and shoes I was off to my aerobics session.

My mind: The calf muscles are paining, possibly due to the stepper workout of the previous session. Maybe you should take the cardio easy today and keep the trainer posted that you are not feeling well.

Providence led the trainer to start with the cardio and my mind immediately started complaining: Take it easy and keep the trainer posted. You are going to aggravate the pain and strain yourself. You have a hectic day ahead.

Slowly she increased the pace of the workout and I was exhausted when I heard her saying "Only five minutes more with cardio. Come on, Push yourself."

My mind: It is okay. You stop. You can't do even one more of anything.

I just ignored temptation and continued with total determination. I told myself "You are not stopping, come what may." But after one cycle when I heard the voice, "Once more" my mind stopped complaining anything as if it realized that I was a lost case and would do only what I wanted. So there was total peace as I continued "Once more." It was as if I had regained all my energy and I didn't want to stop any more.

Then came the abs session with breathing control and I was totally at peace with myself. As the trainer finished with the cool down session I could feel completely rejuvenated. I could feel the gushing blood, the energy all through and most importantly, the peace within.

My mind: Oh! Wow!

For all of us, our mind always tempts us by suggesting shortcuts, softer options, pleasure over pain. It pushes us to a point where we give in. When you start something challenging, mind always searches for pleasure and suggests the easy way out. It portrays that the path chosen by you is tough. You need to brush aside such temptations.

Once you prove that nothing can stop you, it starts working for you. When you see the result, the mind automatically stops complaining and start seeing the positive side. We just have to prove to ourselves that the pleasure achieved is much higher than the easy way out till it becomes a habit. Start working with the mind and see the result it can produce. Let the heart and the mind work in unison.

33

My Child's Best Friend

It was a rainy morning when her mother dropped Anu, aged seven years, to school. They were early to avoid last minute traffic. When you actually plan for a traffic jam, the road seems to be pretty clear and thus Anu landed very early in school. The chairs were on top of the desks. Her classmate Hari arrived and both of them decided to arrange the heavy chairs. They struggled, pushed and pulled to bring the chairs down. In the process, Hari lost his balance and fell down with a chair. His head hit a desk and started bleeding. Not knowing what to do, Anu started crying. Luckily, the teacher came and rushed him to a hospital.

But before that, she blasted Anu, saying, "What did you do? Don't you have any brains? Can't you wait for me to come? Wait till I inform your parents."

Anu was scared and her heart was beating very fast. Wondering what her parents would say, she was even scared to go home. All through the day, she could only imagine the scolding and punishment she would get from her parents. Anything may or may not have actually happened at Anu's place that evening, but the point is that she was least confident that her parents would UNDERSTAND and empathize with her.

All of us have gone through such situations at various stages. It's quite common for children to be scared of their parents. We instill fear in them just to discipline them. When children actually face a crisis, they immediately imagine your angry face shouting and decide not to disclose any unpleasant experience.

Many parents are not even aware that their children are hiding certain things which they are not comfortable discussing with their parents. When your children talk about various things that happened in school, you think they discuss everything with you. But the actual problems may not be revealed, as children feel parents will not understand.

The worst part is that a child is more comfortable discussing these matters with friends and peers, not realizing these peers do not have adequate exposure, experience or maturity to give the right or optimal advice. Sometimes, this advice could even be disastrous.

It is the parents' responsibility to discipline the child. But they also have a responsibility to make the child understand that parents are strict at times only because of their love, not for any other reason. The child should understand the love of parents. Whenever you are upset with your child's behaviour, make it very clear that it is just the act which you don't like, not the child. The child has to see a friend in you. For that, you need to discuss many things other than instructions.

To become your child's friend, it is important that you speak their language and convey a lot of sweet nothings, which make no sense to you but mean a lot to the child. Cartoons, Barbie dolls, colouring sets and masks should be cherished even by you. As the child grows, start enjoying their hobbies, be it rock, dance, actors, etc. Don't shirk when the child asks very private questions. Make it a habit that the child would talk to you for all the solutions it needs. Then the child starts enjoying your friendship which will come handy when the child is in some crisis and you can be sure your child is always on the right track.

34

Is God Partial?

Sometimes I wonder why very few people are recognized as great. Are they very lucky to be born as Gandhi or Teresa or Tendulkar or Rehman? Is it the time of birth or their previous karma? Is it just a distant dream for the remaining population? Is God so partial? If so, why is He God? Thousands of such questions arise within us.

When I was young, my father would say, "I have given you the opportunity and it is up to you to make the most of it." But my inner voice always had an unstated doubt: "Can I?" This firmly created that belief that I'm not among the chosen few and greatness is just a distant dream.

I am sure all of us have dreamt of making it very big in life. Everybody wants to be famous, to be a known figure in society, to mint money and live in style. I don't think there is any exception to it. You can talk to any person and they will share their ambition of starting something novel which will make them very famous and wealthy. While millions have such ambitions, why do only a few succeed? What happens to the rest?

In my opinion, people dream about success, seeing the end product of wealth and fame. As much as the results of the dream are processed, the way to the results is never processed. They ignore the fact that all successful persons were ordinary at one point, but had the self-confidence and will power to face all challenges and succeed. In fact, with opportunities and technology available today, we are in a much more comfortable position than the persons we idolize. Our mindset first needs to change from "Can I?" to "I Can."

We have to start believing firmly that there is a purpose to our life and we are here to fulfil it. Rather than dreaming of name and fame, we should consistently start planning and following the steps which will lead to success. Remember, good luck comes to all as opportunities, but how many are ready for them, identify them and take full advantage when good luck comes our way? Success is a journey, not a destination.

When my son was five years old, he wanted to be a pilot. When he was ten, he wanted to be an astronaut. At fifteen, he wants to be a businessman. The choice of careers keeps changing for many people, with many following a herd mentality. I'm not sure how many even try to understand what excites us, our innate talents, strengths and weaknesses. Identifying one's passion and field of interest is the next step; parents and teachers play an important role in this. Tendulkar is a super success in cricket, but he may not pass the IAS exams. You will succeed in anything only if your heart is in it.

The ultimate goal can be very challenging, but we need to know what to do today to achieve that goal. It could be a small step in the right direction, but it needs to be taken. Every action, every minute of your life has to be dedicated to bring you closer to your goal. All of us dream, but very few act consistently in that direction, and still fewer sustain the action. If you want to beat Tendulkar, you have to be in the field early morning every single day without fail and never ever regret that you miss your morning sleep, social functions, friends' company, etc.

Finally, you have to act continuously with conviction, come what may. Disappointments, failure and rejections—nothing should divert or stop you from your action and your conviction to achieve your dream. This is the process followed by the very few people who change the world and create their mark permanently during their lifetime. We have the talents, but are we willing to do what it takes to become a success? That is the only question which we need to answer

For the question, "Is God partial?" I just smile back, knowing it is with me and not with Him.

35

Do I know what my heart loves?

When a friend asked me to join him for a music concert one evening, I was most reluctant thinking it was just instruments and pure Carnatic music. I said I would not understand the ABC of it because I don't know the grammar of music. I was least interested to go. But as I had no other work that evening, I finally agreed to go with him. Even after reaching the auditorium, my mind was saying that I'll be the odd one out in the audience.

The programme started with the CD release function. With no clue about any of the great personalities on the dais, I felt like an idiot. Cursing myself for being there, I was just waiting for two hours to pass. Then the musicians were introduced and they took their positions for the concert. As they started, I was transported to a different world. I forgot myself and could feel the divine music filling the air. I found myself clapping and enjoying the genius act. The musicians were enjoying themselves with the instruments and the concert was brilliant.

I realized that two hours had passed only when I saw the convener with the mike. I now felt sorry that the magical concert had ended so soon. People say that music can heal, and I sensed the divinity which it can spread. It took a long time for me to come out of the "Aah" feeling this evening had created.

How easily I would have missed this divine experience just because I had a mind block as I never learned the basics of Carnatic music. I would have deprived myself of this opportunity with the mindset that it is all too technical. I realized that music is common to all and you don't need to learn music to enjoy it. You just have to take a small step by exposing yourself to it and get mesmerized. I also noticed that none of the musicians seemed their age and they looked much much younger, which only proved the peace with which they live as most of their life time is spent with the Divine.

Our education system teaches us science, maths, history, geography, literature and their grammar. I now felt that along with these subjects, education should also compulsorily expose children to arts and sports, which should have equal weightage as the existing subjects. Schools do have extracurricular activities, but with minimal weightage. By giving equal importance to science, language, arts and sports, children will be better equipped to choose their careers depending on their talents.

Some parents try giving their child lateral exposure, but much depends on parents' likes and dislikes, their financial strength, area in which they live, proximity to the classes, school timings and parents' convenience to shuttle their children between classes, tuitions and these activities. Giving this exposure to their children remains a distant dream for many parents, and the children grow without exposure to many fields which they might have enjoyed. Fourteen years in school is a long time during the growing years and children to be exposed, given time to see what they love and then given focused training for the activities they enjoy. This would definitely bring out many super stars taking our fame across the globe.

36

My Roots

My cousin Kumudavalli was married to a software engineer in an arranged marriage. The main reason why she happily accepted the match was that he worked aboard and she could also settle abroad. Seeing her keenly anticipating settling abroad, I wondered if anybody could be happy leaving behind their loved ones and the birthplace where they grew up. After settling abroad, I was happy to see her grinning in the pictures she posted showing her new plush surroundings.

After about an year, when she came to India for visa renewal, she visited us, and said she now answers to the name "Kums". I was happy to observe that she appeared more responsible compared to the girl I knew last year. My mother was happy to cook Kums's favourite dishes. We went shopping and I was surprised that she wanted to buy all ethnic stuff. I remembered she always was very western when she was here. When I teased her about her changed taste, her moist eyes communicated more than any words could.

She said, "I have decorated my house in a very traditional way as I very much miss home and our lifestyle. I can't talk my language as nobody except my husband understands it. I feel so jealous when I see you ask your mother to cook any item. Anytime you want, you can visit your parents. I miss walking in the crowded streets just for window shopping. You have no idea how much I miss the hot sun and the cone ice-cream which we had just now. I know their country is better developed, so it is good for my husband's career and for my exposure. But all said and done, the feeling that I'm a stranger in a foreign land never leaves me. I have all material comforts there, but also have an empty feeling which I hate. We can be guests there, but never belong there."

I responded, "Just pack and come back. What's the big deal?" for which she just smiled, so I know she won't come in spite of all that she misses.

The tree stands tall only with the support of the deep roots below. Wherever we go, whatever we do, we belong to the place where our roots are embedded. The satisfaction and peace I get in my motherland is far greater than any money or riches any foreign land can offer. My nation has strengths as well as weaknesses, but all said and done, she is my motherland and I can never leave her for anything. She has freely given me her everything to make me what I'm today. It is my duty for the rest of my life to take care of her at least in every way that I can, to be passed on to future generations.

Let's promise ourselves that we would do everything in our capacity to develop our motherland. It is here that we were born and grew. It is she who fed and nurtured us. When it is time for us to give back, let us not give it to some other nation just because she offers more or looks pretty and rich. Our mother needs us as much as we need her. Jai Hind!

37

Daddy… My Daddy

I have no clue of my dad's feelings when I was born. I assume he had sleepless nights when I was sick, hungry, wet my pants or just wanted to play in the middle of the night. Maybe his heart ached when I fell down trying to walk. But I still remember I used to run to the gate at the honking sound when my dad returned from office. Waiting restlessly while he parked his scooter, I would jump on his shoulder and kiss him. With a smile, he would give me a bar chocolate and I would run to hog it. My mother objected to such pampering, for which my dad would say, "I would do anything for that smile and kiss," and it continued for long years.

I never cared about money even though we were not rich. Anything I needed—an excursion, a cultural programme, a volunteering job, some tuition, a dress, anything—I knew I would get it. My birthday was always celebrated, though he never mentioned or celebrated his birthday. When girls in our family were cosseted rather than encouraged to spread their wings, my dad sent me to engineering college.

When my parents dropped me at hostel, he told me, "I'm not giving you the moon or the stars, but I'm giving you a way to reach them. It is up to you to use these opportunities." I acknowledge that I owe my life to his vision. He equipped me to face life boldly and supported my every decision. Whenever I had problems, he was there to solve it. I learned to be systematic and take up responsibility, not just for my life, but also for people around me. By his actions and attitude, he demonstrated what hard work could achieve; the lessons learnt through observing his life are endless.

Growing up as my dad's pride, I did whatever I wanted, but until I suddenly lost his physical presence, it never struck me that I was marching ahead only with his support and strength. When he departed, I had no clue what hit me and I never wanted to face it. I had never realized that he would suddenly leave us forever. I would have done anything to rewind those moments in life. But now I keep thinking how much precious time I wasted when he was alive. How much I had argued with him to do what I wanted. How many days we just sat together, he with his Sudoku and me with the TV remote. I never realized that his physical presence was an irreplaceable boon and luxury till I lost him. But now, left with just with his memories, I would give my life to have him back.

The father-daughter relationship is unique and a very special feeling. I only wish every daughter realizes the value and blessing of her father while she can still have his physical company. Words like "I love You" are inadequate for the relationship we share. But just to feel contented, express as much as you can during his lifetime What if we are grown up? Who said we have to stop hugging or kissing him? Regret after losing him is futile.

Whatever your age, just go hug him and give him a strong kiss in spite of his resisting, and you can be sure he is still a man who'll do anything for the sake of your smile.

38

Bonding

It was Ayudha Pooja, a festival where we see the divine in everything. The vehicles, the tools which we use, the books we study, basically all things which help us to lead our lives and keep us civilized.

Our office was in festive mood preparing for the pooja. Each of us started cleaning our work places, shelves, doors, windows, fans. People were teasing each other and chatting as they continued to work. We decorated the office with colour papers and the place was vibrating with energy.

A team created rangoli at the entrance with bright colours and flowers. Another team worked on the name board. A couple of them went to the market to buy fruits, flowers and pooja items. A team took charge for the sandal and kumkum dots over all important items: computers, diaries, tools, receipt books, brochures. Everything was venerated with a sacred yellow and red dot. Another team decorated the pooja spot with colour papers and flowers. One team sat packing the puffed rice, sweets and fruits as takeaway prasadam for all employees.

As part of the management team, it was a pleasant sight to watch them work in unison with so much enthusiasm and happiness. Everybody assembled before the deity and the pooja was so fulfilling. Sweets and snacks were distributed and the bright mood united us all. I could see that their personal differences were forgotten that day. There were no barriers dividing them into different departments, cadres, religions, KRA; nothing mattered. It was our office pooja; only that mattered.

We hire a management consultant who comes to teach us the importance of team building. He generally suggests a workshop and we spend so much improving the bonding among employees. We organize office tours, conduct workshops and training programmes to teach people the importance of working together, as a team in unison. At the end of the programme, it could turn out to be yet another routine training with no permanent improvement.

Celebrating festivals at office seems to be a very effective method for team building. It bonds people as a family. When the thought "My office pooja" seeps in, the sense of ownership is taken to a much higher level. The more you bring in this sense of "My office" the more loyal an employee becomes. However this bonding could also be short-lived.

But the beauty of our land is that we have innumerable festivals of all religions and we just need reasons to celebrate. We can start celebrating every festival at office, just not at our homes. The benefits this culture can bring in are intangible. It would be win-win for everybody. The employees who might not celebrate the festival for some reason get to celebrate at office. The bonding among employees improves drastically and improves synergy between departments in their day-to-day affairs.

Most importantly, happiness radiates throughout and increases the energy level of the very place.

Celebrations need not be extravagant affairs. We can define the rituals for office, factoring the amount of time and money that can be spent. The rituals can be simple, but should involve everybody with some task. This would definitely help in bonding between employees and in turn convert the office a happy place to work with. Happy working!

40

Face thyself

A dinner invitation at a close friend's place: Who would refuse? Everybody agreed to be there at 8 pm sharp. Reaching his house at 8 pm, I realized I was the first to arrive. We tried calling the others and realized some were still at their workplaces. I could feel my hunger pangs. God bless my friend's wife, who gave some starters and juice. We started discussing various subjects of common interest. The conversation moved to cleanliness and maintenance.

Wife: He can never keep things in their right place. Shoes never get into the shoe rack, dirty clothes to the bin, or any of his things for that matter. He gives a damn about it and I have to go behind him, picking his belongings to keep the house clean.

Friend: Who is asking you to clean? A home cannot be a military regime. I need freedom and only then I would call it a home. I never asked for a clean house.

Teasing her about her habit of wanting to keep everything clean and organized, he said, "This is also a form of psychiatric behaviour and needs to be corrected." Finally, not wanting to feel more awkward, she left, stating she would set the table.

By 9.30 pm, most of the other guests had arrived. I said, "If you can't come at 8 pm, you could have said you would come at 9.30 pm." The entire conversation now turned to punctuality. Each of them gave reasons for being late, but nobody felt that it was wrong. So what, after all it is only dinner, was the general tone. Now it was my turn to be teased. "Don't rush for dinner. They'll serve it, don't worry." "We are not like you, jobless." and so on. Not wanting to argue, I changed the topic. My friend's wife had organized a maid to stay till 9 pm to help her with serving; with that in mind, she had chapattis on the menu, which now needed to be rolled and made. Now that the maid had left, she was running around.

Did we have a wonderful time? Oh yes. We kept chatting and laughing till late in the night, then bid adieu. While returning home, I felt that his wife was doing the right thing by keeping the house clean. Since my friend cannot raise himself to that level of perfection, he defended himself with some theory. I was right being there on time. Others could not achieve that level of punctuality, hence the bullying. In fact, they should have realized they were being impolite by being late and increasing the workload of the hosts. When you are right while others cannot rise to your level, they justify and pontificate, trying to prove they are right. Anything rightly done needs no explanation.

Nobody is perfect. It is not a crime to be late, disorganized or unorganized. But when you start arguing that you are right, you permanently close the doors of self-improvement, which is not good for you in the long run. When you don't acknowledge your shortcoming, you'll never search for means to correct it. "Yes what I'm doing is not right, but I'm not able to help it," indicates you mean to correct yourself sooner or later.

As much as we appreciate our positive points, let us also have an open mind towards our negative points. A deaf ear, a Nelson's eye, and a closed mind are like Satan which will never allow us to rise to the next level.

www.ingramcontent.com/pod-product-compliance
Ingram Content Group UK Ltd.
Pitfield, Milton Keynes, MK11 3LW, UK
UKHW042015190726
13854UKWH00005B/2292